I promise to guide you, on paths unknown,
and stand by your side, together we'll grow.
I'll help you to learn, we'll read and we'll write,
count stars together, each and every night.

I'll cheer you on, in everything you do,
clapping the loudest, always believing in you.
I'll teach you kindness and how to be strong,
to know what's right and admit when you're wrong.

And as we grow, no matter how far,
I promise to love you, just as you are.
We'll treasure our moments, both big and small,
for our cousinly love is the greatest of all.

Love,
Your Cousin

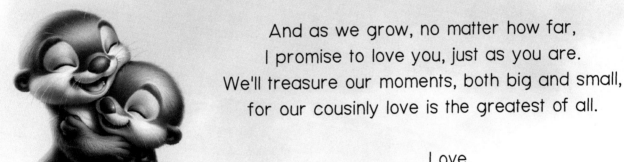

I promise to share my toys,
even when it's my very favorite one.

I promise to keep you safe under
the strongest blanket fort we can build together.

I promise to teach you how to draw, starting
with our favorite animals and magical creatures.

I promise to hold your hand when you take your
first steps, cheering you on with every little wobble.

I promise to show you the stars and teach you
about the moon, making every night a new adventure.

I promise to laugh with you until our bellies hurt,
finding joy in our silliest moments.

I promise to protect you from monsters under the
bed, armed with a flashlight and our bravest hearts.

I promise to be patient with you as you learn,
knowing we all need time to grow.

I promise to introduce you to my friends, making sure you always have a big circle of love and support.

I promise to teach you how to make the best mud
pies, and we'll pretend to eat them at our tea parties.

I promise to teach you about our family traditions,
making sure you feel a part of every special moment.

I promise to always encourage you to dream big,
reminding you that anything is possible.

I promise to share my snacks with you, even if it's the very last chocolate chip cookie.

I promise to make you laugh when you're feeling
sad, with funny faces and goofy grins.

I promise to help you build the tallest towers and
then have fun knocking them down together.

I promise to always stand up for you, being your protector and advocate, no matter what.

I promise to share my books with you, and we'll travel to magical lands through stories and tales.

I promise to teach you kindness and compassion,
showing you how to be a friend to all.

I promise to take you on adventures, from backyard jungles to playground castles

I promise to always celebrate your achievements,
big or small, with cheers and claps and happy dances.

I promise to be a shoulder to lean on, offering hugs and comfort whenever you need it.

I promise to show you the joy of jumping in puddles,
laughing in the rain and chasing rainbows together.

I promise to always have a spare costume for you,
so we can be superheroes whenever the mood strikes us.

I promise to help you catch your first snowflake on your tongue, sharing the magic of winter's first snowfall.

I promise to be there for all your birthdays, helping blow
out the candles and making wishes for the years to come.

I promise to be your partner in imagination, building worlds out of cardboard boxes, fighting dragons or sailing the high seas

And above all, I promise to love you unconditionally, through very up and down. Our bond as cousins is a special gift, one that I'll cherish forever. For in this big world, you and I will always have each other.

a little note for you

Made in the USA
Las Vegas, NV
27 October 2024

10540930R00019